T0123364

"SINUSFELD"

"SINUSFELD"

BY

QUENTIN TERRENTEE-NOSE

"SINUSFELD"

iUniverse books may be ordered through booksellers or by contacting:

iUniverse
1663 Liberty Drive
Bloomington, IN 47403
www.iuniverse.com
1-800-Authors (1-800-288-4677)

ISBN: 978-1-5320-9601-3 (sc)
ISBN: 978-1-5320-9602-0 (e)

Print information available on the last page.

iUniverse rev. date: 05/19/2020

MISSION INFO:

The time: NOW

The place: SINUSFELD, ILLINOIS

The assignment: GET A PULSE ON THE TOWN'S ATTITUDES CONCERNING SEVERAL OF TODAY'S MUCH-DISCUSSED ISSUES

Our operative:

NESTOR NOSTRILDAMUS, WCDS-TV field reporter, interacting with a small citizenry sample to see what its socio-political future may hold

Our voices ot uh... "reason":

- **MUCOUS "MUKE" WALLBURG**, local community-theater actor
- **ASTHMARELDA COLDPLAY**, wife and part-time nanny
- **TAYLOR SNIFFED**, singer with a hit song from her "NOSEMILK" CD, entitled, **LOOK WHAT YOU MADE ME GOO**
- **KINGA "STUFFY" SUTO**, a man who's always so congested, one of his nose-blowing episodes extinguished an intense frying-chicken blaze in his mother's kitchen. Hence the nickname, **STUFFY THE PAN FIRE SPRAYER.**

CRITICAL FINDINGS:

SIMULTANEOUSLY DRINK AND READ THIS BIZARRE, LAUGH-FILLED LITTLE BOOK OF CARTOONS AT YOUR OWN RISK!!! This loopy little masterwork of mirth may send your beverage of choice gushing wildly through your twin inhalation apertures. Continue reading further, and you'll succumb to a strong odor of long-legged humor that will drop you to your **SNEEZE.**

FINAL WARNING : trekking smartly through this aromatic dossier without an ounce of common scents, could result in a delightfully peculiar case of comedy WHIFFlash.

"SINUSFELD"

CREATED BY

QUENTIN TERRENTEE-NOSE

in association with

cHicKEn dOOdLE sOuP

and

ICEBERG TONY

CHRISTOPHER WALKEN NOSE STUNT DOUBLE – **DONNELL OWENS**

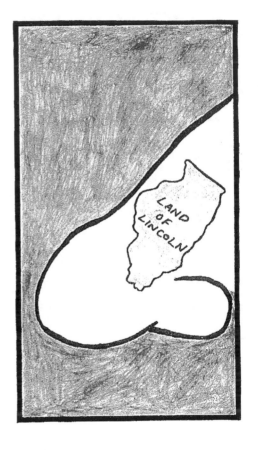

*SPECIAL THANKS TO CHICAGO FLORIST **BREUER HAUTENFAUST**, WHOSE DANGEROUS BUT SUCCESSFUL EXPERIMENTS WITH NUCLEAR RADIATION, PEANUT BUTTER AND JUSTIN BIEBER'S BODY WIG, ALLOW YOU TO WATCH THE BOOK OR READ THE MOVIE AT THE SAME TIME.*

SINUSFELD

BY QUENTIN TERRENTEE-NOSE

SINUSFELD CREATED BY QUENTIN TERRENTEE-NOSE IN ASSOCIATION WITH CHICKEN DOODLE SOUP.
SOMETIMES ALL THE FACE OF IGNORANCE EVER NEEDS IS TO GET A DECENT KNOWS JOB.

SINUSFELD
BY QUENTIN TERRENTEE-NOSE

DON'T GET UPSET, STUFFY. IT'S JUST THAT THANKS TO YOU, I WON'T BE ABLE TO STREAM MY FAVORITE SHOWS FOR A WHILE. I'M SIMPLY WONDERING IF MAYBE IT'S TIME YOU FINALLY GOT SOME PROFESSIONAL HELP FOR THIS DANGEROUS ADDICTION YOU'VE DEVELOPED.

HEY, I WAS FLAT BROKE AND LIFE-AND-DEATH DESPERATE! BUT FOR THE LAST TIME, I APOLOGIZE FOR TRYING TO USE YOUR AMAZON TV FIRE STICK TO VAPE.

SINUSFELD CREATED BY QUENTIN TERRENTEE-NOSE IN ASSOCIATION WITH CHICKEN DOODLE SOUP. SOMETIMES ALL THE FACE OF IGNORANCE EVER NEEDS IS TO GET A DECENT KNOWS JOB.

SINUSFELD
BY QUENTIN TERRENTEE-NOSE

PEOPLE TODAY TREAT THEIR PETS LIKE HUMANS. SO YOUR RICH FRIEND'S HUSBAND IS ALLERGIC TO HER CAT. IT'S CAUSING SO MUCH FRUSTRATION THAT THEY'VE AGREED TO A TRIAL SEPARATION. SHE'S SPENDING $16,000.00 A MONTH TO RENT HIM A ONE-BEDROOM UNIT IN BEVERLY HILLS. HOW DID THEY DECIDE THE HUSBAND SHOULD BE THE ONE TO MOVE INTO THAT SUPER EXPENSIVE APARTMENT?

HE DIDN'T MOVE. THE CAT DID.

SINUSFELD CREATED BY QUENTIN TERRENTEE-NOSE IN ASSOCIATION WITH CHICKEN DOODLE SOUP. SOMETIMES ALL THE FACE OF IGNORANCE EVER NEEDS IS TO GET A DECENT KNOWS JOB.

SINUSFELD
BY QUENTIN TERRENTEE-NOSE

SO THEN, YOU'RE ALL FOR A SOCIETY THAT OPPOSES GENDER IDENTIFICATION. AM I CORRECT, ASTHMARELDA?

YES. BUT ONLY BECAUSE I'LL BE ON TIME FOR WORK A LOT MORE OFTEN, IF NOBODY CARES WHETHER OR NOT I MOW THAT HAIR JUNGLE CROWDING MY ARM PITS AND NOSTRILS.

SINUSFELD CREATED BY QUENTIN TERRENTEE-NOSE IN ASSOCIATION WITH CHICKEN DOODLE SOUP.
SOMETIMES ALL THE FACE OF IGNORANCE EVER NEEDS IS TO GET A DECENT KNOWS JOB.

A

SKILLETFUL OF

STENCH FRIES

FROM THE

POINT OF VIEW

POTATO PANTRY...

IN YOUR OPINION, WHAT MUST WE EARTHLY CUSTODIANS DO IMMEDIATELY TO SAVE OUR FRAGILE PLANET?

"Ship it across several galaxies to live with foster parents."

-- ASTHMARELDA COLDPLAY

SINUSFELD

BY QUENTIN TERRENTEE-NOSE

OKAY, SO TODAY YOU'RE WORLD-FAMOUS SINGING SENSATION, TAYLOR SNIFFED. BUT IF YOU BECAME THIS COUNTRY'S FIRST FEMALE PRESIDENT, WHAT WOULD BE YOUR FIRST ORDER OF BUSINESS?

TO CONVERT THE JOB INTO A SPLIT-SHIFT POSITION, AND SHARE THE RESPONSIBILITIES WITH A CO-ELECTEE. THIS WOULD FREE UP MY TIME TO FOCUS INTENTLY ON GENDER-EQUALITY PROJECTS, LIKE FINALLY HAVING KING KONG PLAYED BY A WOMAN.

SINUSFELD CREATED BY QUENTIN TERRENTEE-NOSE IN ASSOCIATION WITH CHICKEN DOODLE SOUP.
SOMETIMES ALL THE FACE OF IGNORANCE EVER NEEDS IS TO GET A DECENT KNOWS JOB.

SINUSFELD
BY QUENTIN TERRENTEE-NOSE

SINUSFELD CREATED BY QUENTIN TERRENTEE-NOSE IN ASSOCIATION WITH CHICKEN DOODLE SOUP.
SOMETIMES ALL THE FACE OF IGNORANCE EVER NEEDS IS TO GET A DECENT KNOWS JOB.

A

SKILLETFUL OF

STENCH FRIES

FROM THE

POINT OF VIEW

POTATO PANTRY...

IN THESE ENLIGHTENED, SOPHISTICATED TIMES, WHAT IS THIS UNCOMMONLY IRRATIONAL FEAR YOU HAVE THAT MAKES YOU TERRIFIED TO SHAVE ON OCTOBER 31st?

"You need to understand that when my brothers and I lived at home with our parents, every year without fail, those psychopaths would mix candy in with my razor blades!"

--MUKE WALLBURG

SINUSFELD
BY QUENTIN TERRENTEE-NOSE

So MUKE, YOU'RE GIVING UP MEAT AND ANIMAL-BASED CLOTHING AND SKIN PRODUCTS TO BECOME A VEGAN, EH? I'M REALLY SURPRISED.

WHAT???!!! IS THAT WHAT A VEGAN IS? I THOUGHT IT WAS ONE OF THOSE COOL PEOPLE THAT ALWAYS FLASHES THE "V" SIGN WHENEVER THEY WALK THROUGH A CROWD!

SINUSFELD CREATED BY QUENTIN TERRENTEE-NOSE IN ASSOCIATION WITH CHICKEN DOODLE SOUP.
SOMETIMES ALL THE FACE OF IGNORANCE EVER NEEDS IS TO GET A DECENT KNOWS JOB.

SINUSFELD

BY QUENTIN TERRENTEE-NOSE

STUFFY, YOU STREAM YOUR THERAPY SESSIONS LIVE ON SOCIAL MEDIA? WHY?

MY THERAPIST IS LONG-WINDED AND BORING, BUT I CAN'T AFFORD TO BUY AN ITALIAN-LEATHER SOFA LIKE THE ONE IN HIS OFFICE. SO I TELL HIM MY PROBLEM, GRAB A LUXURIOUS NAP, AND LET MY FOLLOWERS TELL ME IF HE COMES UP WITH ANY GOOD ADVICE WHILE I'M SLEEPING.

SINUSFELD CREATED BY QUENTIN TERRENTEE-NOSE IN ASSOCIATION WITH CHICKEN DOODLE SOUP. SOMETIMES ALL THE FACE OF IGNORANCE EVER NEEDS IS TO GET A DECENT KNOWS JOB.

A

SKILLETFUL OF

STENCH FRIES

FROM THE

POINT OF VIEW

POTATO PANTRY...

WOULD YOU PUT YOUR NEIGHBOR'S LIFE BEFORE YOUR OWN?

"You mean as in using him for a shield to protect me from bullets? Yes, and with only the sincerest gratitude - unlike those fake feelings they're famous for in show business."

-- KINGA "STUFFY" SUTO

SINUSFELD BY QUENTIN TERRENTEE-NOSE

THE VERY IDEA OF SLAVERY IS HORRIBLE. CAN YOU EVEN IMAGINE OWNING A PERSON THROUGH LEGAL MONETARY PURCHASE?

NEVER EVER... ALTHOUGH I SOMETIMES LIE AWAKE ALL NIGHT WONDERING HOW YOU WOULD CALCULATE THE SALES TAX.

SINUSFELD CREATED BY QUENTIN TERRENTEE-NOSE IN ASSOCIATION WITH CHICKEN DOODLE SOUP. SOMETIMES ALL THE FACE OF IGNORANCE EVER NEEDS IS TO GET A DECENT KNOWS JOB.

SINUSFELD BY QUENTIN TERRENTEE-NOSE

IF THE CIRCUMSTANCE WERE TO PRESENT ITSELF, WOULD YOU EVER CONSIDER BEING A STAY-AT-HOME DAD WHILE YOUR WIFE WORKS?

I'M SINGLE, ALMOST 50, NO CHILDREN, UNEMPLOYED AND DON'T KNOW WHAT I WANT. BUT I'D HAVE NO PROBLEM BEING A STAY-AT-HOME DAD. MY NAGGING, RENT-HUNGRY PARENTS ALREADY CONSIDER ME EXPERT AT BEING A STAY-AT-HOME SON.

SINUSFELD CREATED BY QUENTIN TERRENTEE-NOSE IN ASSOCIATION WITH CHICKEN DOODLE SOUP.
SOMETIMES ALL THE FACE OF IGNORANCE EVER NEEDS IS TO GET A DECENT KNOWS JOB.

A

SKILLETFUL OF

STENCH FRIES

FROM THE

POINT OF VIEW

POTATO PANTRY...

IS COLD, HARD CASH THE
ANSWER TO ALL YOUR
PROBLEMS?

"Absolutely not! Some of
those problems deal
only in cashiers
checks."

-- ASTHMARELDA COLDPLAY

SINUSFELD
BY QUENTIN TERRENTEE-NOSE

I JUST WATCHED THAT CONTROVERSIAL DOCUMENTARY ON EUTHANASIA. PEOPLE ARE REALLY DIVIDED ON THE TOPIC.

SO I HEAR. WELL, I'VE NEVER BEEN THERE, BUT I'M PRETTY SURE KIDS ON THAT CONTINENT ARE THE SAME AS KIDS EVERYWHERE ELSE IN THE WORLD.

SINUSFELD CREATED BY QUENTIN TERRENTEE-NOSE IN ASSOCIATION WITH CHICKEN DOODLE SOUP.
SOMETIMES ALL THE FACE OF IGNORANCE EVER NEEDS IS TO GET A DECENT KNOWS JOB.

SINUSFELD BY QUENTIN TERRENTEE-NOSE

HAVE YOU EVER THOUGHT ABOUT EXPERIENCING LIFE AS A MAN FOR JUST ONE DAY?

NOT ANY MORE - BECAUSE WITH MY DRY, PATCHY SKIN, DEEP VOICE AND ACID-REFLUX BELCHING, PEOPLE MISTAKE ME FOR MY HUSBAND ALL THE TIME.

SINUSFELD CREATED BY QUENTIN TERRENTEE-NOSE IN ASSOCIATION WITH CHICKEN DOODLE SOUP. SOMETIMES ALL THE FACE OF IGNORANCE EVER NEEDS IS TO GET A DECENT KNOWS JOB.

A

SKILLETFUL OF

STENCH FRIES

FROM THE

POINT OF VIEW

POTATO PANTRY...

WHAT HAS BEEN MANKIND'S FINEST HOUR?

"I'm no good with these quizzes, but I'll say the one we turn back every November to get more sleep."

-- MUKE WALLBURG

SINUSFELD BY QUENTIN TERRENTEE-NOSE

WHAT'S IT GOING TO TAKE FOR SOCIETY TO MAKE ALL THE MADDENING VIOLENCE STOP?

FOR STARTERS, INSIST ON SEPARATE CHECKS WHEN YOU'RE IN A HUNGRY GROUP AND ALL **YOU** WANT IS A LIGHT APPETIZER.

SINUSFELD CREATED BY QUENTIN TERRENTEE-NOSE IN ASSOCIATION WITH CHICKEN DOODLE SOUP.
SOMETIMES ALL THE FACE OF IGNORANCE EVER NEEDS IS TO GET A DECENT KNOWS JOB.

SINUSFELD
BY QUENTIN TERRENTEE-NOSE

A

SKILLETFUL OF

STENCH FRIES

FROM THE

POINT OF VIEW

POTATO PANTRY...

*WHAT DOES IT DO TO
YOU INSIDE WHEN YOU
SEE POOR SOULS LYING
ON THE SIDEWALK?*

*"I should probably be upset.
But I guess it just depends
on the topic they're
lying about."*

--TAYLOR SNIFFED

SINUSFELD BY QUENTIN TERRENTEE-NOSE

WOULD IT HAVE BEEN AN HONOR FOR YOU IF YOU WERE THE FIRST MAN EVER CREATED?

ARE YOU SERIOUS? WHY SHOULD I CONSIDER IT AN HONOR THAT MY PROUD CREATOR IS WALKING AROUND IN HEAVEN, FORCING ANGELS TO VIEW NAKED PHOTOS OF HIS NEWBORN SON THAT CAN PASS FOR A 30-YEAR OLD?

SINUSFELD CREATED BY QUENTIN TERRENTEE-NOSE IN ASSOCIATION WITH CHICKEN DOODLE SOUP. SOMETIMES ALL THE FACE OF IGNORANCE EVER NEEDS IS TO GET A DECENT KNOWS JOB.

SINUSFELD

BY QUENTIN TERRENTEE-NOSE

SO MUKE, I HEAR YOU HAVE BEEF WITH A HUGE ORGANIZATION THAT'S MADE SOME PRETTY BIG HEADLINES.

YOU'RE PRECISELY CORRECT, AND ACTION NEEDS TO BE TAKEN RIGHT AWAY. NOW I ADMIT, I MAY NOT ALWAYS ADHERE TO PROPER GRAMMATICAL GUIDELINES. BUT I'M REASONABLY SURE THE **ME TOO** MOVEMENT SHOULD BE PROPERLY LABELED THE **MYSELF ALSO** MOVEMENT.

SINUSFELD CREATED BY QUENTIN TERRENTEE-NOSE IN ASSOCIATION WITH CHICKEN DOODLE SOUP.
SOMETIMES ALL THE FACE OF IGNORANCE EVER NEEDS IS TO GET A DECENT KNOWS JOB.

A

SKILLETFUL OF

STENCH FRIES

FROM THE

POINT OF VIEW

POTATO PANTRY...

IS THERE REALLY A PLACE WHERE SOME PEOPLE WILL GO TO BURN CONTINOUSLY IN A LAKE OF FIRE?

"Yeah...which is why when I throw a Superbowl Sunday bash, we all chip in for catering rather than trusting my girlfriend to operate my stove."

-- MUKE WALLBURG

SINUSFELD

BY QUENTIN TERRENTEE-NOSE

STUFFY, IF YOU KNEW YOU HAD ONLY 12 MORE MONTHS TO LIVE, WHAT WOULD YOU DO WITH THOSE PRECIOUS REMAINING DAYS?

TRY TO PICK UP SOME EXTRA TIME BY PLEADING WITH HEAVEN TO BEGIN THE COUNTDOWN AT THE START OF A LEAP YEAR.

SINUSFELD CREATED BY QUENTIN TERRENTEE-NOSE IN ASSOCIATION WITH CHICKEN DOODLE SOUP.
SOMETIMES ALL THE FACE OF IGNORANCE EVER NEEDS IS TO GET A DECENT KNOWS JOB.

SINUSFELD

BY QUENTIN TERRENTEE-NOSE

SINUSFELD CREATED BY QUENTIN TERRENTEE-NOSE IN ASSOCIATION WITH CHICKEN DOODLE SOUP.
SOMETIMES ALL THE FACE OF IGNORANCE EVER NEEDS IS TO GET A DECENT KNOWS JOB.

A

SKILLETFUL OF

STENCH FRIES

FROM THE

POINT OF VIEW

POTATO PANTRY...

WHAT'S YOUR VIEW ON OUR NATION'S HEALTH-CARE SYSTEM?

"We definitely need to improve affordability. My grandmother's teeth are so crooked, she got kicked out of her retirement community for throwing gang signs."

-- ASTHMARELDA COLDPLAY

SINUSFELD BY QUENTIN TERRENTEE-NOSE

I OVERHEARD A HEATED ARGUMENT AT A JUICE BAR YESTERDAY MORNING OVER THIS ISSUE: IS A WOMAN'S BODY REALLY HER OWN?

CONSIDERING THE HUGE NUMBER OF COSMETIC SURGERY PROCEDURES SO MANY OF THEM UNDERGO, IT'S NOT VERY LIKELY.

SINUSFELD CREATED BY QUENTIN TERRENTEE-NOSE IN ASSOCIATION WITH CHICKEN DOODLE SOUP.
SOMETIMES ALL THE FACE OF IGNORANCE EVER NEEDS IS TO GET A DECENT KNOWS JOB.

SINUSFELD BY QUENTIN TERRENTEE-NOSE

SINUSFELD CREATED BY QUENTIN TERRENTEE-NOSE IN ASSOCIATION WITH CHICKEN DOODLE SOUP.
SOMETIMES ALL THE FACE OF IGNORANCE EVER NEEDS IS TO GET A DECENT KNOWS JOB.

A

SKILLETFUL OF

STENCH FRIES

FROM THE

POINT OF VIEW

POTATO PANTRY...

DO YOU AND YOUR SIGNIFICANT OTHER STAND EQUALLY AND SIDE-BY-SIDE ON MOST ISSUES?

"I wish we did. But you've seen him. He's so short, one of his ankles is his neck."

-- TAYLOR SNIFFED

SINUSFELD BY QUENTIN TERRENTEE-NOSE

ASTHMARELDA, ARE WOMEN SUPERIOR TO MEN?

YES THEY ARE, WITH THE POSSIBLE EXCEPTION OF SPEED. STATISTICS SHOW THAT MEN DIE FASTER.

SINUSFELD CREATED BY QUENTIN TERRENTEE-NOSE IN ASSOCIATION WITH CHICKEN DOODLE SOUP.
SOMETIMES ALL THE FACE OF IGNORANCE EVER NEEDS IS TO GET A DECENT KNOWS JOB.

44

SINUSFELD
BY QUENTIN TERRENTEE-NOSE

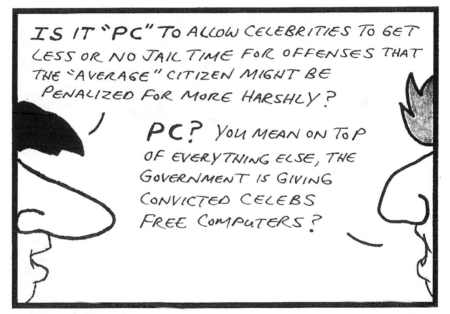

SINUSFELD CREATED BY QUENTIN TERRENTEE-NOSE IN ASSOCIATION WITH CHICKEN DOODLE SOUP.
SOMETIMES ALL THE FACE OF IGNORANCE EVER NEEDS IS TO GET A DECENT KNOWS JOB.

A

SKILLETFUL OF

STENCH FRIES

FROM THE

POINT OF VIEW

POTATO PANTRY...

DO WE PLACE TOO MUCH EMPHASIS ON BEING ATTRACTIVE?

"Yes, and I get so mad about that! On the other hand, my little sister used to be so hideous that when she was born, even our strict social worker let it slide when Mom allowed her newest child to nurse alongside our bull dog's puppies."

-- ASTHMARELDA COLDPLAY

SINUSFELD BY QUENTIN TERRENTEE-NOSE

SINUSFELD CREATED BY QUENTIN TERRENTEE-NOSE IN ASSOCIATION WITH CHICKEN DOODLE SOUP.
SOMETIMES ALL THE FACE OF IGNORANCE EVER NEEDS IS TO GET A DECENT KNOWS JOB.

SINUSFELD BY QUENTIN TERRENTEE-NOSE

SINUSFELD CREATED BY QUENTIN TERRENTEE-NOSE IN ASSOCIATION WITH CHICKEN DOODLE SOUP.
SOMETIMES ALL THE FACE OF IGNORANCE EVER NEEDS IS TO GET A DECENT KNOWS JOB.

A

SKILLETFUL OF

STENCH FRIES

FROM THE

POINT OF VIEW

POTATO PANTRY...

WHEN YOU LIVED ON RACINE AVENUE OVER THAT 24-HOUR LAUNDRY MAT, YOUR EXTENSIVE, RARE COIN COLLECTIONS WERE STOLEN SEVERAL TIMES BY HEARTLESS THIEVES. YET WHEN FINALLY CAUGHT, YOU REFUSED TO HAVE THEM ARRESTED. WHY?

"Because the more rare coins I collected, the greater the nagging responsibility I felt that for some reason, I needed to be available day or night for random customers, in case they needed me to make change."

-- KINGA "STUFFY" SUTO

SINUSFELD BY QUENTIN TERRENTEE-NOSE

SINUSFELD BY QUENTIN TERRENTEE-NOSE

WOULD THE PLANET BE BETTER OFF IF IT WERE ONLY INHABITED BY DINOSAURS?

ARE YOU KIDDING? I GET CHILLS AND DIZZY SPELLS EVERY TIME I THINK ABOUT ALL THOSE WHITE-HAIRED LEGISLATORS.

SINUSFELD CREATED BY QUENTIN TERRENTEE-NOSE IN ASSOCIATION WITH CHICKEN DOODLE SOUP. SOMETIMES ALL THE FACE OF IGNORANCE EVER NEEDS IS TO GET A DECENT KNOWS JOB.

A

SKILLETFUL OF

STENCH FRIES

FROM THE

POINT OF VIEW

POTATO PANTRY...

*WHAT'S AN IMPORTANT
THING YOU WANT THE
WORLD TO KNOW YOU
ABSOLUTELY BELIEVE IN?*

*"I'd like to say following my own
heart. But to this day, I've found
it's physically impossible for me
to walk behind it."*

A

SKILLETFUL OF

STENCH FRIES

FROM THE

POINT OF VIEW

POTATO PANTRY...

CAN YOU HONESTLY SAY YOU HAVE A CLEAR CONSCIENCE?

*"I must have -
I've never ever
needed glasses, but
after all these
years, I still
can't see it."*

-- MUKE WALLBURG

SINUSFELD BY QUENTIN TERRENTEE-NOSE

DO YOU THINK THE COURSE OF HUMANKIND IS ON THE RIGHT TRACK?

YES — FOR AS LONG AS EVERY LIVING PERSON CAN ENJOY WATCHING A REALITY TELEVISION SHOW THAT MAKES THEM FEEL GRATEFUL NOT TO BE ANY OF THE PEOPLE ON THE SERIES.

SINUSFELD CREATED BY QUENTIN TERRENTEE-NOSE IN ASSOCIATION WITH CHICKEN DOODLE SOUP.
SOMETIMES ALL THE FACE OF IGNORANCE EVER NEEDS IS TO GET A DECENT KNOWS JOB.

SINUSFELD BY QUENTIN TERRENTEE-NOSE

SAY, WHAT WAS THE NAME OF ADAM'S WIFE, WHO TOOK THE VERY FIRST BITE OF THE FORBIDDEN FRUIT IN THE GARDEN OF EDEN, WHICH RESULTED IN EVENTUAL DEATH?

WOW, NESTOR. I'M FAR FROM BEING A BIBLE SCHOLAR, BUT EVEN I KNOW THAT ONE. HER NAME WAS SNOW WHITE.

SINUSFELD CREATED BY QUENTIN TERRENTEE-NOSE IN ASSOCIATION WITH CHICKEN DOODLE SOUP. SOMETIMES ALL THE FACE OF IGNORANCE EVER NEEDS IS TO GET A DECENT KNOWS JOB.

A

SKILLETFUL OF

STENCH FRIES

FROM THE

POINT OF VIEW

POTATO PANTRY...

IN THIS NEW MILLENNIUM, CAN WE FREE OURSELVES OF THE DESTRUCTIVE VICES WE STRUGGLED WITH IN THE PRIOR CENTURY?

"Man, I certainly hope so! I remember when I was so addicted to smoking that after my funeral, I wanted my remains to be flown out west so the family could spread my cigarette ashes over the Grand Canyon."

-- ASTHMARELDA COLDPLAY

A

SKILLETFUL OF

STENCH FRIES

FROM THE

POINT OF VIEW

POTATO PANTRY...

WHAT WOULD MAKE YOU
ANGRY ENOUGH TO PURCHASE A
GUN RIGHT THIS MOMENT?

"Delbert and Bertha Suto
shattering my dreams
of finally finding my real parents, by
breaking life-destroying news
to me that I'm not adopted."

-- KINGA "STUFFY" SUTO

SINUSFELD BY QUENTIN TERRENTEE-NOSE

STUFFY, SHOULD FILM STARS BE MAKING POLITICAL STATEMENTS WHEN THEY ACCEPT PERFORMANCE AWARDS?

TO ME IT'S ALL THE SAME, NESTOR. LAST NIGHT I WATCHED AN AWARDS SHOW IN WHICH YOUNG AND HIP POLITICIANS RECEIVED NATIONAL SERVICE RECOGNITION. I WANTED TO HEAR ABOUT THEIR ACHIEVEMENTS, BUT I FELL ASLEEP LISTENING TO THE RECIPIENTS DISCUSS MOVIES AND HOLLYWOOD GOSSIP DURING THEIR ACCEPTANCE SPEECHES.

SINUSFELD CREATED BY QUENTIN TERRENTEE-NOSE IN ASSOCIATION WITH CHICKEN DOODLE SOUP. SOMETIMES ALL THE FACE OF IGNORANCE EVER NEEDS IS TO GET A DECENT KNOWS JOB.

SINUSFELD BY QUENTIN TERRENTEE-NOSE

SHOULD A PERSON BE ALLOWED TO BE PRESIDENT OF THESE UNITED STATES, NO MATTER WHAT COUNTRY HE OR SHE IS FROM?

IT SHOULDN'T MATTER ONE BIT! IN FACT, SOME OF THE BEST PEOPLE I KNOW ARE FROM GEORGIA, ALABAMA, MISSISSIPPI AND ARKANSAS. COUNTRY FOLK ARE THE BEST!

SINUSFELD CREATED BY QUENTIN TERRENTEE-NOSE IN ASSOCIATION WITH CHICKEN DOODLE SOUP.
SOMETIMES ALL THE FACE OF IGNORANCE EVER NEEDS IS TO GET A DECENT KNOWS JOB.

A

SKILLETFUL OF

STENCH FRIES

FROM THE

POINT OF VIEW

POTATO PANTRY...

WHAT ARE YOUR THOUGHTS ON IMMIGRATION?

"Well...they say it's the sincerest form of flattery, but I'd rather be an original than a copycat."

-- MUKE WALLBURG

SINUSFELD
BY QUENTIN TERRENTEE-NOSE

IN THE HORROR HOTEL OF ANGRY PARTISAN DIVISION, WHAT WOULD IT TAKE TO GET A REPUBLICAN AND A DEMOCRAT IN THE SAME BED?

SETTING ONE OF THEIR MATTRESSES ON FIRE.

SINUSFELD CREATED BY QUENTIN TERRENTEE-NOSE IN ASSOCIATION WITH CHICKEN DOODLE SOUP. SOMETIMES ALL THE FACE OF IGNORANCE EVER NEEDS IS TO GET A DECENT KNOWS JOB.

SINUSFELD

BY QUENTIN TERRENTEE-NOSE

SINUSFELD CREATED BY QUENTIN TERRENTEE-NOSE IN ASSOCIATION WITH CHICKEN DOODLE SOUP.
SOMETIMES ALL THE FACE OF IGNORANCE EVER NEEDS IS TO GET A DECENT KNOWS JOB.

AND

FINALLY...

ↄↄↄↄↄↄↄↄↄↄↄↄↄↄↄↄↄ

SINUSFELD BY QUENTIN TERRENTEE-NOSE

COULD A NATION COMPRISED SOLEY OF MEN EXCEL WITHOUT WOMEN?

ABSOLUTELY — BUT IT WOULDN'T HURT IF A FRACTION OF ITS CITIZENS COMMUNICATED VERBALLY TO OTHER MEN USING HIGH-PITCHED VOICES.

SINUSFELD CREATED BY QUENTIN TERRENTEE-NOSE IN ASSOCIATION WITH CHICKEN DOODLE SOUP.
SOMETIMES ALL THE FACE OF IGNORANCE EVER NEEDS IS TO GET A DECENT KNOWS JOB.

A

SKILLETFUL OF

STENCH FRIES

FROM THE

POINT OF VIEW

POTATO PANTRY...

WHETHER IN OLD OR MODERN TIMES, RELATIONSHIPS CAN BE TOUGH WITHOUT COMMITMENT. BECAUSE OF YOUR TYPICAL LACK OF WILLINGNESS TO COMMIT TO PRETTY MUCH ANYTHING, YOU ASKED YOUR GIRLFRIEND FOR A TRIAL SEPARATION. ANY NEWS TO REPORT?

"Uh, yes. There was a trial separation -- marked with extreme ugliness and violence. Because during the course of that trial, she and her friends sentenced me to hang."

-- KINGA "STUFFY" SUTO

ABOUT THE AUTHOR...

*QUENTIN TERRENTEE-NOSE is well known for poking fun at society, political division and spotlighting corporate misconduct with his off the-wall projects, including **PULP FACTION, RESERVOIR DOGMA, KILL a Capitol Hill BILL**, snack-meat obsession drama, **JERKY BROWN**, his award winning documentaries about corruption in the fruit industry during a devastating crop shortage in Hawaii, **MANGO UNCHAINED** and **THE HATEFUL ATE**, a church-choir competition that started a war in the action-packed **INGLORIOUS PASTORS**, and the powerful, groundbreaking masterpiece about leisurely obsessions, incompetence and deadly mishaps involving power tools and lumber, **DUNCE UPON A TIME IN HOBBY WOOD.***

*Mr. Terrentee-Nose is currently undergoing intensive psychiatric therapy due to guilt because, even though he is married soley to his imagination, it pressures him nonstop for a legitimate church ceremony. Send good wishes to him at **LEGITANDBYTHEBOOK.COM.***

"SINUSFELD"

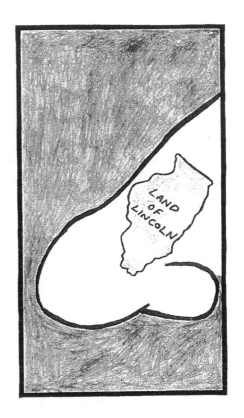

CREATED BY

QUENTIN TERRENTEE-NOSE

FIND MORE INFORMATION ABOUT WHAT WE'RE UP TO ONLINE AT LEGITANDBYTHEBOOK.COM. DROP US A LINE TO SAY HI.